KB189460

Cold Reading

Cold Reading

A collection of new poems by Kang Hyebin
Translated by Rieux (Hyunji) Choi

콜드 리딩 강혜빈

K-Poet Series 044

ASIA

Contents

COLD READING

Cold Reading

You are possessed
The face of a shaman

God says, beautiful, big-eyed.
Lips smell of warm jujube.

In Sajik-dong where gods of Land and Grain
    bid farewell. Where the alleys have aged the
    most in Seoul. I sit facing a blinding white
    god. Drinking the soul mass long simmered
    smooth and low. Dark and sweet. ⌜Empty it
    before the soul cools down of its innocence.⌟

The sugar cubes in the glass bowl turns to

powder in the blink of god's eye. Icy winter
wind blows into the neatly empty folding
screen. Powdered sugar in the palm and
drawing a circle makes doughs the shape of
a human. Prayers perishing when leaving the
hand. Not yet, a little more please. Maybe
three days of delay but. God does not step
back. 「I have chosen you. Going insane was
inevitable......」 A black deer passes behind my
eyes as god's lips gently close.

The deer's belly is wet with moisture. Treading
on the mushrooms spread along the forest
path. Jumping left and jumping right and

circling the willow tree, tottering awhile,
trotting away. As my eyes follow the blunt
tail disappearing. Overshadowing the tea
ceremony with god. A white teacup clatters as
if possessed.

Holding the handle, my whole body is
trembling. Incense scent spreading like
electricity. Frozen lake in the teacup smacks,
cracks open. The lake lifts up a dizzying chill
and. Dead family members ooze out through
the thick ice walls split in two. Grandma,
grandpa, great aunt, dad, auntie's auntie,
faceless babies, uncle's uncle, future me. The

tip of my nose feels bitterly cold.

Again god says, beautiful big-eyed. ⌜Come
with me. I will make you fly.⌟ God stirs the
remaining tea with such long, white little
finger. The table narrows down snugly. God
moistens the lips. Cold tongue. Cold teacup.
Cold tea. Cold spirits. Cold books. Cold
reading. Cold blood. Cold corpse. Cold
poop. Cold love. Cold ear. Cold fins. As
my hand places itself on god's forehead, my
eyeballs turn white, frozen.

Everything becomes visible.

happyphobia

Say you're sad three times a day
Forest, Fragments, Finale

Hide a shattered bottle in your t-shirt
Cheese, Whiskey, Alprazolam

And grin
Wide

Why are you at my house?
Without legs, even

New Gwisins are delivered day after day
Please leave just a long face on the doorsteps

We are with these edgy heads
Taut at 3 and frown at 15

We hang damp blankets and
Eat watermelons naked
Planking is just too easy
Shall we kiss lightly too?

Someone's there on a dead TV
Swamp, Bias, Leaf flute

Cannot lie down on the rim of summer
If too hot, might cry as well

Things seen
Only when stepped aside, stealthy

Anxiety, erased itself of shadows
Turns on briefly, fades away
Then channel adjustment begins
A cold hand seizing my ankle, every other step

Learn the weather for the ceiling, peeling red
Hand fan, Shaman Belll, Escitalopram

If some strange nose pops out from your pot
Say: ah, how so lonely

Then forget it

Practice stretching your legs, earnestly
Stare the girl in the mirror down
Train whistling in the clearest tone
Tears of blood would mean losing

If you beat me
I'll give you my lfe of today

I wish some lost, fresh Gwisin barged into my
    house

Bewitch me

Lift me high

Make me choke

Let me touch you

How so sad am I today

Pok-Poong*, Ping-Pong, Pang-Pang!

*A Korean word for tempest.

Superconductor

Today is the appointed Wednesday, Doctor
Thesedays Geubun does not come often
In my airy life, I wait
for Geubun
Sound of water, eyes closed
Drops of air floating downward
Geubun…… makes me dance
Shows me future, undelivered
Makes me love the person I wish to kill
Carves the smile on my worn wrist
Shows me all the mutants in the world
In squares, in rooftops, on emergency stairs
We do the crooked steps
To cuddle failures

To continue the queer dance

To rise to our feet with broken knees

May we connect our sloshing tears

And jump rope with them

Geubun...... makes us dance

Shaking the heated glasses

Screaming until we taste blood

Laughing until tears burst out, Pang-Pang

Lying face down on the ground

Until we vomit

Until we vomit

Makes me miss my father, died early winter

The pale young man fades away little by little

The breath hits the window

Such a hazy Wednesday, Doctor

I can sleep when I'm dead

Even the street rats are asleep now

Nipping a knife, preparing a bowl of cold water

Counting the strands of hair on the pillowslip

I wait for Geubun

A mushroom sprouting from the dry pot

A wall clock falling down on its own

A dead battery signal

A stranger's face on the mirror

Are they Geubun

Showing me hallucinations

Giving me the ear of a dog

Impossible to prove by modern medicine

Geubun used my hollow body as a paint bucket

Until the water became filthy

Until the water became foul

Geubun washed the soaked brushes over and
over

To dirty those innocent yesterdays

Do you know, Doctor

What it's like to be painted airtight

What it's like to have apnea,

Do you know?

Geubun becoming a baby, rotting away in the
belly

Becoming a chunk of paint

My baby, left only as a name like a ghost......

Not even crying, no tossing and turning

As the mirrorball flashed far away

I danced

Pretending not to know future, though I saw it
   all

Licking a neck after strangling

I have wondered every Wednesday

Until when do I have to be healthy?

May I look down from a high rise?

I don't want to be some great one

I want to be any one

Can it be this boring?

Can it be earth free riding?

I want to have a baby

Can I live like others do?

Shall I love Eonni, Oppa, Hyung, Noona,
    everyone?

Can I too become gray-haired?

Only such stupid feeling left after curiosity gone

Only such dull feeling of a rubber eraser......

It's just about time, but

Geubun is not coming

A metallic sound comes from the waiting room
    speaker

My conductor body

Might work as ear swab

Both of us would feel satisfying, you know......

We would suck up every black on earth

In the Wednesdays' magnetic field, you know

Becoming Orange

Orange, a species of citrus

Were born a healthy Korean, 3.2 kilograms

Orange, all round and firm, both heavy and
tender

Were glad they could be born and die in the 21st
century

Orange, realizing the messiness of the world the
moment they were born

dreamed only to die a *natural death*自然死

Orange were the first child of oranges who gave
birth to oranges

They had three younger siblings but

Two of them fell sick and died, one lived, and
they were very close

Orange had bumpy skin

And damp heart

Most of them were neutral but

Sometimes they opened up wide, posing as a
   butterfly

Sometimes they became ripe marmalade

Sometimes a sincere lover

Or an ice cream store worker

A delivery person or a pilot

Or a petty kumquat

Open parenthesis

Pronounce Orange strangely

Close parenthesis

A sip of water

Roving and scratching belly

Consciously swallowing saliva

Consciously blinking eyes

Consciously feeling the position of a tongue

Consciously like a human being

Open parenthesis

Orange period

Orange comma

Orange exclamation mark

Orange question mark

Close parenthesis

Silence, silences

Save this document?

YES / NO

The heart's muscles are involuntary

The mind is not in the heart

But in the delivery box thrown out in front of
the door

But in the leftover ice cream lid

On the airplane cargo container

On the wife's lovely forehead

To live in the body of an Orange, you see

Only Orange would know

When I'm feeling Orange

I spread out a map and dot the stores I do not
know

The mind of a stranger

Only strangers would know

The mind of a person who lives alone

Only a person who lives alone would know

Such honest loneliness, just for the day

Just the spare amount for one person

Becoming Orange juice

Becoming Orange jam

Orange peel Orange comfiture

Orange cake filled with sorbet

Orange Givrée

Orange cream cake glazed

Becoming Orange segments

Wondering my use

Before getting serious

All anyhow Orange.

Becoming just a timid

Just a sincere

Strange Orange.

Infinite Proliferation

a group of persons sit in a darkened room there is no person who invited only those who have been invited people with unfamiliar voices and enough hunger the owners of confirmed IDs person 1 stands up and shouts, i am a freak then person 7 follows one more person, three more persons stand up then one person, five persons silently grope for the doorknob in the dark i am a freak too, me too, me too a storm of applause and the sound of two lips touching and parting the persons left the room slightly damaging the things the things broken hastily their tossing and turnings fill one part of the room only the prepared freaks remain, sitting together and sharing dry humor and swallowing sounds at times the voices cut off and continue like Morse codes there is an outsider freak who just listens from the beginning to the end the freaks takes on the appearances of freaks a freak who draws paintings a freak who counts money a freak who writes books a freak who speaks Spanish a freak who drums with bare hands a freak who gazes out to New York afternoon a freak who gives a recipe for a chickenless steamed chicken dish a freak who does not know how to ride a bike a freak who became a poet after wearing a white lab coat and observing onion skins under a microscope at the age of twenty a freak who talks about an island herb a freak who asks to use the herb as the title of their novel a freak who broke up with their lover who is afraid of receiving gifts a freak who sighs hearing the story freaks, freaks

What a pity

freak 11 asks, worrying in written language, why are you still awake? what about you? i am made to stay awake i could not even turn myself off since i was born without a power button what a pity, how unfortunate i hope you sleep without any dream then i could sleep in peace and you next, you after, you front and back could all sleep tight too you might even never wake up too i believe in the hypothesis that we were all designed to only talk about sleep with each other but it was not proven freaks permitted to sleep turn off their mics the last ones remaining share white noise until they grow tired, until they grow pale old, the room remains there remembering birthdays and deathdays one after the other, the freaks form freaks' room

Blue and Squashy Water Bottle

Are you a green activist? he asks
Whenever seeing the water bottle

No, though I have beans and oatmeal
Two times a week

Stained thoughts I have
Couldn't tell anyone
Only two times a week……

I sit in a black chair, chest out
Wondering if it's okay to be
So open, so proud

He, demonstrating the pose with a bit dry face
Says, anatomically

(Touch here)

The front and the back are connected
When the front opens, the back closes
The more you open the front, the less it hurts

Mouth and anus
Anus and mouth

Sometimes I wish to close up all the holes
I wish I could solder the word 'goo-meong'

It would be splendid if the 'goo' and 'meong'
   fuses
As the molten lead fully flows and spreads
Meong-meong! Like a dog blind to the heat
Like you and I did
Unable to breathe
Sweatless and fuzzy!
Not crying nor excreting
Just like a closed, blue and squashy
Water bottle……
Waiting for the day I am quietly opened
Holding my breath until my face explodes
Holding, holding, then bursting out
Dying at the moment when

The holes are the happiest on earth

As if falling into deep meditation

No, mouth and anus

Anus and mouth

Blood poop! Ppoojik!

Students giggling at poop stories

A thirty-year-old teacher who still bursts into
    laughter

At nose picking stories

And other holes

Humans are nothing more than sponges poked
    with holes

True green is human extinction

Thinking about the end of the world

I grope for bulging wing bones
The rattling equipment smells like iron

His armpits are sleek
So sure to give a big, open hug

He sits in a black chair
Packs his proud shoulders

The person with round shoulders
Keeps feeling small
Swallows bad words in the throat
Hesitates to request for side dish refills

I wasn't always like this from the start

Your shoulders are too rounded
Be open, be proud
Until you wonder if it's okay

Let my pride be your misery
I count up, refreshed

Shoulders go back and forth, in and out
Rather than up and down
Like clicking the knock-type ballpoint pen
I put my shoulders in then bring them back

One day, when the rain was drumming on the
   window
The water bottle vanished without a trace

Stunned: where did I put my
Blue and squashy water bottle?
I needed water

Instead I only used a paper cup until it became
   mushy
I only helped it die gently, but

Are you a green activist? he asks
Refusing, reducing, recycling......

That kind of movement, you know

Shoulders away from ears
Take a long knife and stab deep
Close your ribs
Feel the ripping sensation
Where is your water bottle?
Do you eat some chicken now?
You work even on Saturdays?
Stab with a knife

Shoulder packing:
The act of bringing the wing bones back and
    down

A water clock

Fixed by a thumbtack

That is me

Sook-ee Wants To Be a Subject

When called Sook-a,
Close your ears

Come on, Sook-ee?
Change your name
Draw a small mole under the lips
Plant a lemon tree in your front yard
Learn British accents
Burn down your waddling closet and
Drive a silver sports car
Swim in the morning
Order a ballet suit with sleek hands
Forget about yesterday's Sook-ee

Yes, you are Anna
Anna, right?

You are getting scarily coy

No, Young,
You are Young, right?

Your face is blank

Sook-ee is looking for a small brown bag
Inside the small brown pocket are her pills

Sook-ee, in a crooked posture

With a twisted neck

Wants to lie down and play online Rummikub

Without anyone interrupting her

Ignoring the rice pot and the microwave

And the wide open fridge door

And all the machine noises

Wants to kill time

Wants to get a gentle bouquet of flowers

And let the hot water running

Spilling down the tub

Wants to scoop up a crème brûlée just for her
And drink a cup of Affogato

Wants to cross legs
Wants to wake up all limbs stretched
In a king size bed

Again, when called Sook-a,

She is asleep before she knows
She calls for the boss, in the middle of snoring

What the hell is wrong with you Boss
What did I ever do wrong

Ssi-bal!!

A strange rhythm forms
With Sook-ee's snoring and
Jingling of pearl mobile
Jumbling up

At the peak of sleep
She plunges

Woof!

Sook-ee likes rainy days

She doesn't like meat in soup

Sook-ee gave birth to a white baby girl on the
    rooftop
As for Anna, she would pick out her favorite LP
    at midday
Young-ee carries out emotional labor even on
    weekends

Sook-ee hates cream bread
In fact, she likes boredom and monotony

Sook-ee is made
Just for Sook-ee

Sook-ee never understands
What is typical of Sook-ee

The small brown bag is nowhere to be found

When the potatoes sprout and leaves grow
When trees form a forest
When the forest coils around Sook-ee
When she is tamed by the forest

On the living room floor
A flower resembling a Dokkaebi* bat
Pops out of nowhere

*Dokkaebi are deities or spirits from Korean mythology and folklore, deemed to possess extraordinary powers, often accompanying a magical bat.

Anna Likes the Summer Parka

Snugness of the parka
Seam of the parka
Glistening gold buckles
Above all, the brand logo
I have never had

I like them

Summer closet. Heavy rain showering.
Summer closet. A refuge of shrunk sweater.

What are you doing?
Looking at the parka

Looking at

What Eonni left

The heart I couldn't wear, couldn't throw away

(Actually, Anna is gazing over the back side of the closet)

I only wore it once

The parka not mine

The parka I hid it in the corner

In case someone might see

Carol of July

Makes the hollow limbs dance

Jingle bells
Jingle bells

Outside the window
Headlights flash
Bloom like morning glory

If you could bring forward winter
Eonni,
Will you come see me?

A soul soft as cotton wool
Splits into pieces

When you boil it hot

I imagine a warm and plump belly of a goose
I have never touched in my life

Faint smell of naphthalene......

(Anna's closet adds up to three)

Will you come see me
On Christmas day?

I'm using this t-shirt thrown out after one
  season

As a feet towel

Blouse dress mini skirts
Designs so shoddy
Still alive after ten years
Trends turn like plague

You can't even throw this out
You bought this on sale
There's no space now
Don't say throw out
You didn't even know it's here

(Anna quarrels with the closet)

Clothes not yet dead
Flutter like zombies
Swarms of black bean leaves

Jingle bells
Jingle bells
Jingle all the way

Eonni, when you come back
Will you give me the parka?

Will you live as dark as possible
Without boiler, without love?

Summer closet. Swelling pancake.
Summer closet. Thick lint balls.

Carol of July
Makes a lonely person lonelier

What are you doing?
Looking at the parka

Spotless purity of the parka
Vanity of the parka
Firm waistband and
Above all, the brand logo

More real than real

I like them

(Anna goes into the closet)

Broken doorbell rings
Too loud it rings

Jingle
Jingle
*Jingle-au-war**

Summer parka

Stands from morning till night

Like someone left without a place
Like a tree cut off of roots

*A Korean phrase used at something gross, creepy, or weird.

Return and Order

Water tank broken into pieces
Those four silences

A child reading a water-proof book and
A woman wearing a blue ball cap

Above the woman's head hangs
A dead crocodile

Crocodile
Crowds of crocodiles......

Crocodile
Crowds of crocodiles are......

My hair bushy as a black poodle
My heart harmless as a penguin
My legs merciless as a kangaroo

Another brown poodle washes the dishes
It's hard to find the same species nowadays

Clam lamps lighting up the walls
Indoors wrapped by a dome-shaped glass lid

A name written in red letters
Inside a snow white ashtray

⌜ Obettou Matsumoto sang—!
Please stop smoking⌟

Today's face is of summer's awning
Today's glee is of exhausted feet

Mom, I don't have energy left now

Transparent pencil cap gently
Protects the head

You shouldn't poke on random people

Halibut with sunken cheekbone walks by

Teolle Teolle*

Fish in one-room flats clamor out
There's no soundproof at all
There's no roof, too
Poop from above pour down

Fins smiling when it rains
Never in deep sea rain would come

From the eyes of a child
Looking down at the tank

Fall

the

te

ars

of

blood

The disease is common in thesedays kids, you

know

Worms crawling in front of your eyes
Tongue ripped into three
Luminous mushrooms sprout out of necks
Bat's wings on the armpits

This is a New Humans' city
Where recycled trash feels emotions

Please return
Your dishes

* Korean mimetic word describing one's walk in a depressive
mood, close to powerless swaggering.

Afternoon, Sunscreen Suggested

Gong Sa Sam Goo!
*Gong Sa Sam Goo!**

Someone yells outside the window

In the afternoon classroom
Are tilted postures and

Watermelon colored water bottle
Wormwood colored powder med

Chalkboard and broken chalk
Longhorn beetle appearing on the ceiling

Pondering all sorts of greens
I shift my position on the chair, briefly

Low flying airplane sound
Particular Matter (PM) moderate

Piercing
Roar......

Moderate means not outstanding
Nor inferior
A so-so level

I take off a mask

Then back on

Gong Sa Sam Goo!
Gong Sa Sam Goo!

Arithmetical progression
Relative pronoun
Cubit equation
Should have p.p
Probability distribution
Initial sound rule
Circle and asterisk

Teacher, have you ever drunk nosebleed?

Has your voice come back?
Have you ever loved?

Piercing
Piercing

Afternoon airplanes
Have a hunch of summer's height

The sight I've first seen at four years old
My reflection in a puddle

Four-wheeled bikes and
Heat haze hovering above asphalt

Vines climbing the black bars and
A flat ball

Peace of country apartments
People living, not much happening

Waking up it's metropolis
With students living in the same apartments
A so-so teacher
Solves so-so problems

Cough
Cough

My soul runs like snot
I think there's someone inside my body

A classroom without curtains

One student brings up a long umbrella
Teacher, please kill that cockroach

Sunlight bites my right arm

Gong Sa Sam Goo!
Gong Sa Sam Goo......

Car owner does not appear

The voice trails off

Wrong answer notes pile up on the desk

Wrong
Gong Sam Sam Goo
That's longhorn beetle

* Gong(0), Sa(4), Sam(3), Goo(9) stands for numbers in Korean.
The four numbers refer to the vehicle number plate.

Squares of Yours

All of you, get up
Set up a square house

(Sound of desks rattling)

Don't push
Don't slap
Don't crush
Don't poke
Don't win
Don't rob
Don't scream
Don't cross the line
Don't anticipate

Roll and roll your body so you

Be round

Raise your hand one by one

Lift your feet two by two

If not at least

Lift the candy wrap with your mouth

Wait, no matter what

Wait

Share split-stained chips

Don't forget to say thank you

Tell only white lies

Close the front and back doors tight

The need to pee or poop

Being hungry

Being bored

Insults or swearing

Things repressed

Things blurting out

All of this uncontrollable being-alive

Wait, endure all of it, every single thing

Damn!

Building up butt strength

For two hours you should

Only defend your squares

Only your rights well, okay?

(Little feet busily move)

Achoo

As Yo-on sneezes
Se yells

Come on, hide with your arm!
You spit!

Swoosh
Kids' eyes are fixed
Se swings a pencil
Whoosh Whoosh
Yo-on covers her ears

Loud!
Loud!
You're so loud!

Se always grasps a yellow sharp pencil always
Like a baton

Students, I will read a story about a giant exiled
from the earth being cursed by burning down
a town's old tree See those blackened knees of
neighbors over there? The giant had no friends
It could not tell a lie The tree had lived for more
than five thousand years It was so big you could
not embrace it Then it was burnt down vanished

It became ash black as a crow What should we feel about this? *Teacher don't discriminate giant Teacher who cares I got mosquito bite in my eyeball yesterday Teacher can I take off my glasses? Teacher I don't know the right face for the blank space Teacher I got a call from my dead mom Teacher I had a nightmare today Teacher can I eat now? Can I mix it? Can I rip it? So what? No it isn't! No I hate it Please don't Teacher*

Teacher Teacher Teacher Teacher Teacher Teacher
Teacher Teacher Teacher Teacher Teacher Teacher
Teacher Teacher Teacher Teacher Teacher Teacher
Teacher Teacher Teacher Teacher Teacher Teacher
Teacher Teacher Teacher Teacher Teacher Teacher
Teacher Teacher Teacher Teacher Teacher Teacher
Teacher Teacher Teacher Teacher Teacher Teacher
Teacher Teacher Teacher Teacher Teacher Teacher
Teacher Teacher Teacher Teacher Teacher Teacher
Teacher Teacher Teacher Teacher Teacher Teacher
Teacher Teacher Teacher Teacher Teacher Teacher
Teacher Teacher Teacher Teacher Teacher Teacher
Teacher Teacher Teacher Teacher Teacher Teacher

Achoo

Achoo

Yo-on…… could not stop

Like a runaway train

Turning somersaults

Like a whiz sneezer

Chi, Chi, Chi, Achichichi Achoo

Forming rhythms

Coating Se's face with

Saliva

Yo-on came from outer space

Sometimes her pigtails surge up to the ceiling

Glittering scale sprout from her forehead

Aha! She cries out

Kids' faces crumple
They melt down behind the chairs or
Hide beneath the desks or
Move farthest away from the center possible

All of you get up,
Get out of your home

(Big feet kick the floor)

Se prowls around
Se wants to control feelings

Se wants to wear logical pants

Se cannot understand a crying person

Se wipes her dry face and

Freaks out at the smell of saliva then

Slaps her face

Too hard

Yo-on suddenly bursts into tears

Like an audio, left with only volume 0 and 100

Full swing

Properly, if possible

Full of sorrow

Weeps the tears, then

Outer space listens

Se yells, screeches

Come on, hide with your arm!
Your tears splash!

An eraser pops in the air
Split in half
Punctured
Tattered
Smelling of sugar
Cracked like shedded skin
Transformed into magic poop powder

Green nosebleed droops on Yo-on's philtrum

and

(Sound of dragging on time)

Achoo
Achoo

Squared time crumbles down
From the edge, from the good student
From the obedient roof
One by one

Every step on the floor
Leaves the paint patterns spread, not yet dry

The sweet smell of sweat filling the classroom
The dizzying smell of fear......

Kids start to look for their masks
Unattended erasers and masks all jumble up
White things have become filthy, proud

When the teacher erases the date on the
    blackboard
And turns around

All gray the kids' hair had turned

House on the Far End, 6th Floor

When Saturday afternoon arrives
Everyone wonders

What shall we have for dinner?
Yeah, what shall we have?

How about curry
With sweet potatoes in
Griddle old pumpkin pancakes too?
Why are you laughing?
(emoji)
I bought green onions from mart
I'm bringing leftover rice bread
So how about curry

I fried pak choy in oyster sauce

Sweet potato has sprouts

Omg

(emoji)

Who's not coming today?

You need pick up?

Who wants to go to cafe tomorrow?

Did someone just swear?

Iwaru says

Shush

I'm recording

Everyday v-log is playing

In the house on the far end, 6th floor

A cat lives there
Aged over forty in human terms
Iwaru lives there
Aged over forty in human terms
Iwaru is a coffee and vinyl lover
Lives single and
Willingly opens up his home

Huku is the name of the cat
Huku meaning
The lucky one

The ears, like a secret note
The tail, like a question mark
Are flapped

Every Saturday evening
Shoes and trash pile up
In Huku and Iwaru's house

Huku neither runs nor
Climbs up to a higher place now

Shuntaro, taller than Iwaru
And nineteen years younger
Searches all over the small room

⌜ Get these thrown away shoes
All 275 size⌟

Every weekend in the house on the far end, 6th
   floor
Opens a flee market

Shuntaro wears a pair of white sneakers
With the backs pushed down
Buys a linen shirt he sold long ago
At half the price

Iwaru says

Take it off a minute

Anna flings the apron
Hina wears the apron
Curry dissolves just like curry

Anna looks like Hina, but
Hina doesn't look like Anna
What a mystery

Ido pops out of the closet
And takes Shuntaro's sneakers off
But not a chance

Without Anna and Hina
The house doesn't smell delicious

Last summer, Ido became
Allergic to cat hair

Summer with Huku and
Summer last year is not the same

She sneezes two times
Rubs her eyes and
Looks at Huku
A far cuter mister with white whiskers

Curry laps all golden
Only served just enough
Bowls emptied
Water glasses mingled

A person trying to turn off TV
A person trying to stay tuned to a channel
A person mixing the rice
A person scooping up like a sand castle
All gather in a circle
And play rock-paper-scissors

Today's dish-washing is
The amount the loser could not accept

The auction starts at 10,000 won

Hundreds of videos are
In Iwaru's camera but
There's no contents
Run out of capacity
Only full of laughter
Everyone in such a good appetite
Slicing a whipped-cream cake
And techno-dancing
Sometimes a guest sits awkwardly
Garlands from Shuntaro's birthday
Reused on Hina's birthday
Masako and Gyuta Sang are there

Who passed away together
The year before last
They all look like a happy family

Masako, who gave birth to them
Rests on a kitchen chair and
Gyuta lies on a sofa

If you believe it that way
You see it that way

Ido, just because
Her eyes are itchy
Rubbed so much

Lets the tears flow

Though Huku really never runs
Just sleeps on and on

Prince Stationery Store Alley

Recommended sales offer for beginners: Where it gets longer at nights and shorter on days

Left alley

My friend Chunji liked to jump rope with
cut out electric cords Chunji's little sister
Chunma used to ride a four-wheeled bicycle,
dragging the eyeless Ddosoon-ee Chunji and
Chunma giggled with cigarette ash smeared
on their faces I had to wear worn-out clothes
to go see them Chunji and Chunma did not
grow older, stuck in nine and five year old
until I became twenty

Middle alley

Mister Soft-tofu clanged the bell on the evenings
  but no one came out Renting a room under
  the crescent moon Mijoo looked for her
  father every night Appa Appa Please Appa
  Her slant eyes slanted more as the scream
  knocked on the doors house to house but no
  one came out I used to peek on her house
  hiding in my veranda and her shadow, like a
  full grown tree roamed around Mijoo seemed
  to be hanging on the ceiling

Right alley

Red-haired Hwayeon and Yeonhwa's house
was on the ninth basement floor where the
doors only open when you crack a calabash
with your head or spray red beans all over
your body Ajumma said, out of a sudden,
during the meal, Leave this place behind, and
thrusted a black talisman into my mom's ear I
braided Hwayeon and Yeonhwa's red hair into
three pigtails but there was no rubber band to
tie the ends Still Hwayeon and Yeonhwa was
beautiful like candle drippings, without any
expression Ajumma hid her daughters in the
closet and dug her house down every day to

not become a shaman

*Choices for good children: Where it gets steep in
winters and loose in summers*

Beginning alley

Monday. A boiler house dog bit my leg
while I was trying to throw out a sound
door Tuesday. I snooped around a screwed
up video store and got lost in the rain
Wednesday. I buried my old father Thursday.
I drew my deskmate's butt and ripped the
paper down the toilet but it was discovered
at the school faucet Friday. I jumped from

a stranger's house rooftop Saturday. I sold
a friend pulling my arm to the church to
a dogman Sunday. I ignored my mother
walking by the school then Monday. I came
back to the ending alley and said I am sorry

Virtual Happy Hour

Congratulations. To your brilliance. Your
loneliness. Your being alive. Congratulations.
To our last day. To the big blue lilyturf
dried dead. To the endless summer. Happy.
Happy......

Haepari* Island was the place we met. Where
you can breathe underwater. An untact date
on a virtual beach. Happy time listening
to electronic music and taking screenshots.
Swimming by the two characters is a blue
Haepari. Thick Haepari. Square ghost
Haepari. Forest Root Haepari. Bucket hat
Haepari. Rhopilema esculentm. Mooreom

Saengseon**. Woobak Mangtae***. Jellyfish. Medusozoa. Kurage.**** Haewall.***** Mool-i-sil-maeng-ee. Mool-loot. Mool-eo-eum. Mool-woo-seul. Mi-woo-seol. Haepeng-ee. Huipari. Haeporae. Haebarae. Saeparee. Gaeporee. Haeparang-ee. Happy. Happy......

The name splits like drops of water. You threw away your weapons. You threw away your shield. You threw away your glittering potion. Slime tails and Snail shells too. All of them, you threw away. Empty bodied. You gazed at your empty pockets. At the transparent sadness. At the UFO of the sea. At the breakup virus.

It's been 8,760 hours since you logged in.
Please rest a little.

I want to touch. The soft water inside a monitor. The voice of seaweed. In a movement just for float away. In a natural way, sinking to the bottom when stopped. Instead of saying I love you. Let's be dumped in deep sea. So no one can find us. Let's die on a hidden map. They say Haepari grows another leg, same size, when its leg is cut off. They say it lives forever if it is not eaten away. That's a bit scary. You speak in bubbles and. I send green whispers. Happy birthday.

* A Korean word for jellyfish.

** A Korean term for jellyfish as food. Saengseon is a term for fish as food, and Mooreom refers to someone who is weak or limp, rather teasingly.

*** A Korean dialect of jellyfish, mainly used in Jeju Island.

**** A Japanese term for jellyfish.

***** A Korean term in Chinese characters for jellyfish. Hae means ocean, and wall means moon. Jellyfish is sometimes called Haewall (sea moon) because of their moon-like shape when floating in water.

Chamber Music with Warm Air

Listening to a hummingbird snoring

piu piu
...... piu piu

Pearl mobile sways

⌈I hear someone using a knife
Somewhere⌋

He says politely and then
Always
Clears his throat

I'm the one who

Didn't wish to hear
A hummingbird snoring, but

The sound of blue pearls clinking
Small scale chamber music
Beautiful as a scratch

⌜You are too
Far away now⌟

I only tilted my posture a bit
With a receiver at the same spot

Still he senses the future by breathing sound
Prepares for the worst scenario
Such a prophetic human

Though I am only here
Just like this

After the snoring recital comes
Schumann Mendelssohn Brahms Tchaikovsky

The speaker, understanding the intention of the
    examiner
Dawdles and

Turns off the circulator

Inefficiently speaking:

The speaker crawls to the edge of the bed
  and presses the power button on the air
  circulating household appliance, stopping the
  circulation of air which creates unnecessary
  noise

The algorithm manager, wondering what to
  have for dinner
Only plays hummingbird clips

A long lost friend
Became a mother of three
I am secretly
Rooting for her life

Schumann's piano quartet
No. 1 in D minor

poco piu
poco piu

A little more
A little more

The sound of air deflating

From his noise one time

piu piu

...... piu piuuu

Let me hear just three more times

I say and he

Let me hear three more times

ma non troppo

But not too much

Hummingbird is the smallest bird in the world

Efficiently speaking:
Clear your throat once

It can float still in one spot

He swallows a yawn
He practices the AI-replica song of a singer
He imagines a future where artificial womb is
    commercialized

poco a poco
Gradually......

rubato
At a free tempo

Mobile makes sounds
Swaying

Making sounds and
Being there

Orchid Heaven

Bite me foreign. With your wet front teeth.
Step on the green. Where you expand. There,
glittering downhill. Are they us? My new-
grown uvula tickles. Something more like a
squishy leaf. Helplessly spitting, right there. A
handle turning to your side. Greasy trees.

Were they us?
Were they really us?

Today I want to do Maybes with you. Smile. Like
a sweet Wednesday. Good weather. Weather or
Wether. Capricious like a broken A. I'm close
with rough sketches. Covering over rude days.

Shall we nourish an immature However? The ankle I want to love passes by.

Dear my square-eyed Cloud. If only I could cherish your crying face. If only my shoulder could pronounce rieul*. Relax and Sex part in parallel ways. I'm glued in the air. Mae Mae. I don't know such a thing as collar. Is this button a rational one, or? I don't know such a thing as hole. I know how to rub cheeks. Why should I know how to love. Dear my long-nosed Cloud.

Bury me light. With pointed goodbyes. Roll

up the green. Where you remember. There, a prayer sprinkling down. Are they us? An unspeakable color fills up under my tongue. Something more like a dirty nap. A narrowing dream, on and on. Just as a condom is a condom, even in English. A helpless traffic light.

Were they us?
Were they really us?

* A Korean consonant which stands for sounds for [r] and [l].

Healing

Stress Chronic Fatigue
Heal with Massage

When I stopped by
Unable to ignore the sign

You said this is the right path
Showing the red dot on the map

Healing means applying moisture cream
All over the body and mind

Someone who lives north said
It's nice to live there, wet and cold

Is that possible at the same time?

I live south so
It's sunny and clear today

Just like summer indeed, but

I blow my breath on the camera
And wipe with my elbow

Hoping to see clearly but
The street lamp light slips down

As if it has been waiting all along
As if to show
The real light

You ask me What
Have you been shooting

Clasped hands grow awkward
Getting loose little by little

I'd decided I'd say I don't know
Only when I really don't know but

How can I pretend the innocent smoothly

CCTV in a residential street
Red eye blinks
Then disappears

A 13-minute walk to the station
The last train will arrive soon

You said this is the right path
Right

But still you looked around

The music was a bit too relaxed

From the intro of a game where
You have to finish cooking in five minutes

Whenever we felt lost
We sang, walking

The music
Without lyrics
All off-key

I didn't hear the chorus
Since we were hurriedly parting, but

I felt like crying

It was a moment I started to believe

A wet and cold summer exists, indeed

Cemetery Park

I walked among the names

On a side road
At a park as well as a grave

I remembered one name

A name pronounced
Without lips bumping

When you sleep deep, it's because of deep
sadness

You said so

To me sleeping longer

Seedlings are
Trees beside the grave

Third meaning according to a dictionary

I pick up tree nuts from the ground
Through the half open purple shell
Is a whiff of grass after the rain

I'll never ever be friends with someone who
    plucks flowers

Park keeper approaches and says
It closes at five

He wears black sunglasses
In his hand hangs
A hose, water dripping from the end

I had an appointment at five
Now gone

Cemetery Park opens from ten in the morning
Free of charge

Even the keeper rests on Sundays

Ruby Kendrick

Horace Grant Underwood

J.W. Heron

Mary Scranton

Kaichi Soda

Rosetta Hall

Ernest Bethell*......

I walked among the names

Tombstones made of stone
Height 76cm Front 30cm Sides 13cm

Running the fingers over them
Hollow
Sunken bullet holes

An old couple sits on a bench like still life
Lovers taking a wrong turn go back

A scene I feel a little hungry

Restaurants around the Cemetery Park:
(0.13 km) Golden Cheese Tart
(0.16 km) Byeongcheon Aunae Soondae Jokbal
(0.17 km) Passage
(0.26 km) Notdog And Fries Night

(0.27 km) Before Gray

I had a wish to meet someone
Now gone

I remembered a name
Three times

A QR code is there
On the Grave 19 but

Today feels like Sunday
Strange

* All of the names are foreign missionaries who established universities and Christian associations in Korea in the modern era. They are buried in Yanghwajin Foreign Missionary Cemetery, located in Mapo-gu, Seoul.

Yilan*

Open the curtains, and the sea wells up like a
    pudding
A cable car floats through the air
We weren't afraid of the heights

Hoping to learn a dance in fashion
We go

Down
Down

Camelia blooming on wire fences
Azalia rashly stretching out
Gosh, I like flowers more and more

Beauty tickles my eyes

Vietnam, Mongolia, Thailand, Laos
They say mixing water and paradise
Makes your blood thinner

Gosh, it's so much fun even when lost
Live mode cameras and
Decibels respecting others
Small waves, big waves

A squashed penguin
A Turtle with different expressions

A dog with one eye dropped
Hoping to gather camelia blooming on the
    ground
We go

Up
Up

In a city of unpredictable weather
Two black people roam around

So alike yet so different
Blood shared
You, flawless, hating insects and

Me, flawful, hating backpacking
You, fond of a death number
Me, speaking clearly
While sleeping

Five hours are all we have
With a giant heart
Plodding

Do not look above

Cam cam.**
Wind gently pushing at our backs
Cam cam.

Tenderness of potato salad and

Hinoki scented lotion.

Fragrant excitement of the travelers

Pointy-eared dogs and

Saggy foliage plants.

Incense smell.

Cam cam.

Buying the long-hanging

Fortune

Driving down the coastal road

Towards the night hotel

Having a home to go back to tomorrow

Thinking about a broken up lover

While drinking non-alcoholic beer

We'll be back when we're old together

Leaving young love and sadness and broken
   promises
On a sandy beach
With no one there

* Yilan is a county in Taiwan, located in northeastern province. It
is pronounced "Gî-lân" in Taiwanese.
** Cam cam is an adjective in Korean, meaning absolute pitch
dark, sometimes referring to a state of hopelessness.

Winter Solstice 冬至

Hairs of the night droop along
Arcades at midnight
Long and full

I read the unlit sign, squinting
The shop is there but seen only with eyes closed

Closed Today

The person who misread
Bad Luck Tapa* as Bad Luck Party

Waters a dying plant
Strokes a dry hand of a lover

Gladly
Enters into the hairs of the night

The depressed afternoon
Just wouldn't get out of bed

Take a warm shower
Take a walk under the sun
Otherwise……

The doctor says but
The doctor is more depressed than I, actually

The afternoon falls

Into a deep, long winter sleep

On the way back
Past the closed shops

The execution ground, a wooden building
Stands inside a 5 meter height wall

A poplar tree is lying
Under the black cloth

On the black cloth falls white snow
A black cat leaves
White paw prints

The poplar tree, standing still for a hundred
    years
Gazing at the deaths

Finally lies down

Fortunately
I had two legs so
I come back and
Eat instant Padjuk**

The sweetness of artificial sweeteners
I can feel it as a living being

Wishing to be a Gwisin having eaten well
I chew Sae-al-shim*** hard
I will die a natural death, no matter what

Like an old dead poplar tree
I want to be swayed by winter nights

There are more bad people in the world
Than bad Gwisins, you know

Shoo Shoo

Anxiety, slouching on the couch

Shrugs its shoulders and
Seeps into the sink

Bubbles by itself and
The bowl rattles

One out of three is a bad man
If the world is worth living in
Maybe I am the demon

I count the hairs of the night
I see my sleeping face

Just wouldn't wake up, no matter what

* A Korean word for doing away or beating, usually of harmful things.

** A Korean traditional red bean porridge, usually served on winter solstice.

*** A birdseed-sized ball made of glutinous rice flour or sorghum powder and put in Padjuk, pumpkin porridge, etc.

Vladivostok

Moonless night, the taxi roamed around
    the streets and landed in an unfamiliar
    neighborhood
Let's go back now, I said

You ask a passerby walking a dog for directions
Though our destination is in fact right in front
    of you

The dog and the passerby is safe The dog
    and the passerby looks alike as mother and
    daughter The dog and the passerby both
    wears fluffy hats They wave They paw They
    try hard to explain They draw dots lines

surfaces to somehow understand They fluster
a long, long time The dog licks the passerby's
ankle with a big tongue The passerby gives
her white ankle without a word

Some glittering headlights flash by and

Suspicious shadows roam around The sound
of firecrackers fizzing without notice We
are from Korea We are harmless A stranger
approaches and borrows cigarettes and lights
We are from down below We are women
Someone shuts the window as if smashing
We'll go back soon We talk in our sleep

Such a boring, cam cam night view
Surrounded by bushes and steel bars

It's bulbous like a grave, I relax as I climb up the
hill I cry with my square lips and you laugh
with your triangle lips Nothing happens when
you cry and then laugh but I feel something
will happen any minute Dark lovers are
leaning against a rail close to a cliff, hugging,
seemingly a lump from a distance...... You
hugged me just like them We'll do anything
what everyone else does, you say and I say,
why do humans whisper love in high places

Traces made by yellow lights

I spread my fingers out and move them slowly

Someone speaks Korean in the dark

POET'S NOTE

I became a bucket of water chosen by poetry

On a blank sheet of paper
Bladed sharp

Often I fainted
Gone mad or insane......

Into an empty body
Flows crazy love

The sound of a god whispering

Sorry
I ruined everything

POET'S ESSAY

⌜ *"Cold Reading." Reading coldly. Or a highly advanced psychological technique to read the inner thoughts of someone without prior knowledge. It is like a human-computer grasping the past and present of human beings and predicting the future. The one who performs cold reading is called a 'cold reader.'*⌟

This book is a record of a poet's being alive.

I had dreams since I was very young. Every day. Dreams of flying over the vast open sea, watching my grandmother's back as she walks to her grave, saving a snake trapped in a barbed wire fence, falling asleep on my dead father's lap, climbing an enormous blue mountain, exorcising a demon which has escaped from a book, throwing a nuclear bomb capped in a water bottle, meeting ancestors in Hanbok, becoming an attractive man, participating in the Korean War, being cremated, staring at a burning house, becoming a soldier, becoming a spy and dying without anyone knowing......

I was sick for no reason. Numerous tests were done, but I was never given a diagnosis. Healthy family members died away one after another. Close people disappeared from my island. Everything I did went wrong. Everything in the world felt trivial, as if it were beneath my feet. Someone always appeared and saved me every time I became alone.

One day, my body felt so light. I felt like I could float up in the sky any moment. As if every drop of blood had been drained from my body. Fingertips started to disappear, transparent. It was a rainy night. I kept suffering from tinnitus. Unknown voices continued. I couldn't sleep at all for days, or when I laid myself down to sleep, a black figure loomed over me.

I prayed to all the gods I knew.
Please let my future be quiet.

Flash, when my eyes open.

Ecstasy.
The poem begins.

COMMENTARY

A Dance of Becoming a Jellyfish, Hugged by Ghosts

Sung Hyunah (Literary Critic)

Kang Hyebin's poetry is unceasingly innocent even in the face of the gruesome cruelty of the world. When sorrow wraps itself around the body layer upon layer, the poet, not suffocating under the weight of the crushing sadness but instead enjoys the texture of the soft, cloud-like sorrow, is all the time cheerful. Kang Hyebin dresses in layers of puffy tragedies and becomes a jellyfish herself to overlap with more transparent ghosts and glittering souls. It is not that she isn't sad. It is not that she runs far away from sadness and is cheerful by herself throughout. She "felt like crying" ("Healing") and transcribes a line from the movie "Moonlight" (2017) in her prose collection: "I cry so much sometimes I feel like I'm just gonna turn into drops."

However, she never drowns, even when overwhelmed by the rushing world of tears; she feels the flow of it as the sea. She whispers: "Let's swim until we use up all the fins we have left in us" (One *Day Suddenly, Affectionately,* And publishers, 2024, p187), to touch and caress each other's pain. We smile as we read Kang's poems, as she idly flows and become flexible and smooth to embrace "all the mutants in the world" ("Superconductor"). And then we realize that "[H]umans are nothing more than sponges poked with holes" ("Blue and Squashy Water Bottle"). The characters in her poems feel relieved as they let drops of blood and tears, sweat and sadness flow out of their body's holes, but also feel poignantly lonely in the unfilled hollowness. They also are delighted letting in all sorts of strangers through the open crevices. Through witnessing these beings, we, as readers, sway between gladness that we could flow into each other to fill the void and flooding sorrow on the anticipation that these waves touching our flesh will never dry up.

Kang Hyebin once declared that she would be a container for beings like herself, those who fade like ghosts in a world where they must constantly prove themselves and ask for permission to love, asking "Is it okay / To love?" ("Rainbow Engraving", *Night's Palette* , Moonji Publishing, 2020). In her second collection of poems, *Future Humming* , (Moonji Publishing,

2023) she summons a god who has been called to kick out the love of 'freaks' as abnormal, breaks down the conventional wisdom on monotheism, gaining a bolder approval as: "The Great God Says to // Love / Fully" ("Future Mutant").

She has also brought a strange future with a new gesture formed with non-humans, those who are humans but not deemed as such, and non-adults who are deprived of the opportunity to grow up and do not wish to become just another adult. In her latest collection of poems, *Cold Reading*, Kang Hyebin continues to dance through "a movement just for floating away" ("Virtual Happy Hour"). She gladly flows, welcoming wholeheartedly those who have shed their tears and are left with nothing but the ripples.

In Kang Hyebin's poems, 'I' is visited by "New Gwisins" ("happyphobia") everyday. The narrator does not act as a psychic medium to listen to Gwisins' stories or to embrace their pain. Nor does she perform a requiem service through "being possessed", which is commonly believed to be a poet's quality as an intermediary and a mediator. Instead, she waits for them to rush in, fresh and bright, and to bewitch her. Rather than listening to the wretched life stories of Gwisins and relieve their rancor, she learns a salpuri (exorcism) dance that no human can dare imitate from these spirits, who are not only grief-stricken but also lighthearted, who has learned that grief and joy could coexist. In fact, "[t]here are more bad people in the world / Than bad Gwisins" ("Winter Solace"). The 'I's who are more often than not blamed as witches or demons know exactly what this dance means, desperately flowing and swaying just to become their true selves.

This tender hospitality turns the souls who have been recklessly blamed as disasters or falsely accused into welcome guests, coming to comfort another being. Literally, Kang's poems turn "Bad Luck Tapa as Bad Luck Party" ("Winter Solace"). So the longest and darkest winter day, Winter Solace (or Dongji冬至 in Korean) becomes a joyous day when comrades (or Dongji同志 in Korean) who are forced to be non-humans and sometimes inevitably branded as evils visit and stay a longer while. In her poems, this world is a profoundly mysterious place, "a park as well as a grave" ("Cemetery Park"). Thus, it is a place where walks, grave visits, death, happiness, cheerfulness and sorrow all could coexist.

In this way, Kang Hyebin deeply understands the paradox of juxtaposing the seemingly incompatible propositions. One wonders how such insight is possible; is it because she is a poet, a photographer, a lecturer, an a tarot master, fending her life as multiple bodies simultaneously? We might not know everything, but one thing is clear: that she is enduring both a busily bustling life and slow death, passionate love and fierce hate simultaneously. Not only does she endure, but daringly enjoys it. Following the footsteps of Kang Hyebin, who cries and laughs with light face resembling water droplets, we are not just afraid of the collapsing world. We feel what awaits us is more than just imminent destruction.

When we breathe in her poems and inhale all the spirits contained, we are reborn with a squashy, huge heart. This hard-won heart embraces the round blanks, and "[i]nto an empty body / Flows crazy love" ("Poet's Note"). Our heart becomes so full, so light.

PRAISE FOR
KANG HYEBIN

The poetic narrator in *Night's Palette* is a confessing "single person" but almost always splits into "two selves" or forms a dialogic structure in various ways, confronting or push-pulling each other. This composition becomes a profound form that meets the quality of a poetry collection. For Kang, it is the "queer" ontology that brings about the split of the subject. For example, the "one person" who confesses here sways between "Eonni and Hyung" ("Rainbow Engraving"). Kang Hyebin's first collection of poems confronts this issue head-on, sheds light on it from various angles, delves into it in depth, and opens up new horizons. (...) *Night's Palette* is powerful in many ways. The poems with different titles seem to mingle in the "palette" of this collection, blurring the boundaries. Sometimes it felt as if the collective impression is scattered across the poems, rather than each poem collected and bound together. The images the entire collection give are more overwhelming than individual poems themselves. Kang Hyebin's next poems will start from this collection.

– Kim Haeng-suk, "Arriving at a Declaration through Confession - Secrets, Rainbows, and Blue Blood," *Munhak Dongnae* Fall 2020.

While the first collection of poems, *Night's Palette* , showed the process of "Genesis," deconstructing the values and language of the world in which the subject resides and forming a new world, *Future Humming* depicts the process of "Exodus," resisting the real and overcomes hardships as the narrator "often is honest and often despairs, but walks bravely in the end" ("Sorry, But I'm Not Dead Yet," *My Life and Health* ,

Jaeum&Moeum Publishing Co., 2021, p105) towards the future. In this collection of poems, Kang continues to take a new gaze at the "body" that must adapt to the conventions of language, also unfolding the sensation and speculation of discovering others.

– Yum Sun-ok, "A Way to Welcome a World That Does Not Welcome," *Lyric Poetry & Poetics* , Fall 2023 issue.

Kang Hyebin's new poems show the depth of thought about the world's principles in which we exist and the ways of life in it. The poet shows a metaphysical attitude towards the world and things at a very theoretical sense; such philosophical interests swarm with various themes such as the dualistic composition world principles like yin and yang, sun and moon, the Apollonian and the Dionysian world, as well as the art of time such as night and day, moment and eternity.

– Hwang Chi-bok, "The Power of Thinking,"
Yeolinsihak , Winter 2017

Queers and girls in *Night's Palette* relativize the familiar world order based on their "strange" bodily sensations. I would like to add that the deft camouflage they display is not simply a play skill, but a technique for surviving in that world. They fight, love, and grow up, dreaming of a moment when "I don't have to prove that I am me", when it ceases to "feel like a miracle that we are alive" ("Minimalist").

– Kim Bo-kyung, "Strange or Unfamiliar,"
Literature and Society , Summer 2020

K-POET
Cold Reading

Written by Kang Hyebin
Translated by Rieux (Hyunji) Choi
Published by ASIA Publishers
Address 445, Hoedong-gil, Paju-si, Gyeonggi-do, Korea
(Seoul Office: 161-1, Seodal-ro, Dongjak-gu,Seoul, Korea)
Email bookasia@hanmail.net
ISBN 979-11-5662-317-5 (set) | 979-11-5662-729-6 (04810)
First published in Korea by ASIA Publishers 2024

*This book is published with the support of the Literature Translation Institute of Korea
(LTI Korea).

K-픽션 시리즈 | Korean Fiction Series

〈K-픽션〉 시리즈는 한국문학의 젊은 상상력입니다. 최근 발표된 가장 우수하고 흥미로운 작품을 엄선하여 출간하는 〈K-픽션〉은 한국문학의 생생한 현장을 국내외 독자들과 실시간으로 공유하고자 기획되었습니다. 〈바이링궐 에디션 한국 대표 소설〉 시리즈를 통해 검증된 탁월한 번역진이 참여하여 원작의 재미와 품격을 최대한 살린 〈K-픽션〉 시리즈는 매 계절마다 새로운 작품을 선보입니다.